RUFUS THE SCRUB

DOES *NOT* WEAR A TUTU

BY
JAMIE McEWAN

ILLUSTRATIONS BY JOHN MARGESON

DARBY CREEK PUBLISHING

To Caitlin

Text copyright © 2007 by Jamie McEwan
Illustrations copyright © 2007 by John Margeson

Cataloging-in-Publication

McEwan, James.
Rufus the scrub does not wear a tutu / by Jamie McEwan ; illustrations by John Margeson.
    p. ; cm.
ISBN-13: 978-1-58196-060-0
ISBN-10: 1-58196-060-3
Sequel to: Whitewater scrubs. Summary: Rufus finds himself involved in both the football team and a ballet class. Despite the teasing from his friends, the ballet lessons may just save the football season. 1. Middle school students—Juvenile fiction. 2. Athletes—Juvenile fiction. 3. Football—Juvenile fiction. 4. Teasing—Juvenile fiction. [1. Middle school students—Fiction. 2. Athletes—Fiction. 3. Football—Fiction. 4. Teasing—Fiction.] I. Title. II. Ill.
PZ7.M478463 Ru 2007
[Fic] dc22
OCLC: 70692091

Published by Darby Creek Publishing
7858 Industrial Parkway
Plain City, OH 43064
www.darbycreekpublishing.com

Printed in the United States of America

1 2 3 4 5 6 7 8 9 10

1-58196-060-3
978-1-58196-060-0

CONTENTS

CHAPTER 1

PAIN IS

It was only the first day of football practice, and already Coach Stone was turning purple.

Maybe he was purple because it was such a hot day. Even up on the football field, high on the hill, there was no breeze. But Coach Stone's purple face probably had something to do with the way he was yelling at everybody.

"Hit him!" He shouted so loudly that his voice echoed off the far hill. "Tackle him! Rufus, you look half asleep! Biff, hold onto the ball! You guys look like you're playing ring-around-the-rosy! Play *football*!"

"Wow," said Rufus to his friends, Willy and Dan. "What's he so worked up about?"

But Coach Stone heard him.

"What am I so worked up about, huh, Rufus? I'll tell you what I'm worked up about. We graduated more than half our team. I've got to teach a bunch of newbies how to play. And I've got to try to whip the rest of you scrubs into shape!"

Coach Stone paused and looked back and forth, his head jutting forward like a vulture looking for prey.

"The Bears never had a losing season," he went on, "and I don't plan on having one this year. That means we're going to have to work extra hard! All right, take a lap! Take two laps!" Spit was flying from his lips as he yelled. "Run! If I see anybody dogging it, he'll do another lap!"

In the locker room after practice, the players were almost too tired to change clothes.

"Am I really going to do this another year?" asked Willy. "Another year on the bench? And practice . . . oh, man, I hurt all over!"

"'Pain is weakness leaving the body,'" said Dan. Dan was always quoting stuff he'd read on posters or in magazines.

"I think pain is just pain," said Rufus.

"'Pain is temporary. Pride is forever,'" said Dan. "This year we're going to be great."

"We're still the smallest guys out there," said Willy.

"Not me," said Rufus.

"Yeah, but you make up for it by being so slow and klutzy!" said Biff from the next row of benches. Biff was small—only Willy and Dan's size—but he was a star player. "You're all scrubs," said Biff. "Every one of you."

"Scrubs try harder!" said Willy.

"Okay, fine, *be* scrubs," said Biff. "Sit on the bench. Cheer me on while *I* get all the touchdowns. No skin off my nose."

"Except when Rufus tackles you," said Dan. "That might take the skin off your nose."

"If he ever catches me," said Biff, grabbing his backpack and jogging out of the room.

The three friends were silent as they dressed. After a minute, Rufus said, "Gosh, maybe my mom was right."

"About what?" asked Willy.

"Tell you later," said Rufus, pulling on his shoes. "Got to go!"

CHAPTER 2

COTTON CANDY

Rufus was used to being the biggest guy in his class at school. But this was ridiculous.

He hadn't realized that the other beginners were going to be, for one thing, all girls. And for another thing, all under eight-years-old. Some of them didn't even come up to his waist.

Somehow, even though this was a beginning class, all of these tiny little girls already seemed know what a "*plié*" and a "*relevé*" were and what "turnout" meant. How did they know? Were little girls born knowing stuff like that?

And when it came to doing "*pirouettes*," they whirled around like cotton candy being spun onto a cone.

But when Rufus tried to spin, he lost his balance and almost knocked over a couple of little girls.

"Sorry!" he told them.

"That's okay," they said, laughing.

Ms. Farine, the dance teacher, was a skinny young woman with lots of energy. She dashed around the room, correcting the little girls and showing them how to do better. When she passed Rufus, she smiled and said, "Very good Rufus! Remember to point your toes!" No matter how clumsy Rufus was, she always smiled and complimented him.

At first Rufus found this reassuring. But after a while, it started to weird him out.

After class, Ms. Farine gave Rufus an even bigger smile than usual and asked,

"Will we see you tomorrow?"

"Sure," said Rufus. "Why not?"

CHAPTER 3

CHOOSE!

At practice the next day, Rufus went up to Coach Stone between drills.

"I've got to go, Coach," he said.

"What?" said Coach Stone. "We've still got fifteen minutes to go, Rufus!"

"Yeah, but I've got to go early to be on time for my ballet class."

Coach Stone stared at him with bulging eyes. "Ballet class!?"

"Yeah."

"Ms. Farine's ballet class?" asked the coach.

"Yeah."

"Rufus, nobody takes that class but a bunch of eight-year-old girls."

"I know. I was there yesterday."

"No, Rufus," said Coach Stone. "You can't leave early for ballet. That's ridiculous. You need to be out here hitting! You've got to learn to hit hard!"

"But Coach, it's—"

"No! I won't have it! You're a football player, Rufus. You're going to start on this team. And you're not going to miss practice for ballet!"

"I have to go," said Rufus.

"No way," said Coach Stone, shaking his head. "You're going to have to choose. Ballet or football—you can't do both."

"I have to choose?" asked Rufus.

"That's right," said Coach Stone.

Rufus looked around. By now, the whole team was listening.

"Well, I guess I won't see you tomorrow then," said Rufus, and he trotted off the field.

"Wait!" Coach Stone shouted after him. "You can't! We need you! Come back tomorrow, and we'll talk about it!"

CHAPTER 4
TUTU?

In the morning, before classes, all anybody could talk about was Rufus taking ballet.

"The scrubs wear tutus!" yelled Biff as he came down the hallway. "I want to see it! Rufus in a tutu!"

"You wish," said Rufus. "Sorry, Biff, only the girls get to wear tutus."

"What's a tutu?" asked Dan. "It's no fun being insulted if I don't understand what it means."

"A tutu is one of those ballet skirts that puffs straight out," explained Rufus.

"I want to see Rufus wear a tutu at football practice!" yelled Biff.

"What do you really wear at dance class?" asked Willy.

"Tights and a sweatshirt," said Rufus.

"Good enough," said Biff. "Come to practice in pretty pink tights!"

Rufus couldn't care less what Biff said.

Later at lunch, Clara sat down beside Rufus and started asking him questions about ballet.

Clara was a tall girl and a really good soccer and basketball player. But somehow she had become one of the scrubs, too. She had gone kayaking with them last spring.

"Whatever made you think of ballet?" asked Clara.

"My mom suggested it," said Rufus.

"Your mom?" asked Willy.

"Yeah. I was complaining that I was really clumsy, and she said, 'You should take dance. I'll pay for dance lessons.' So I decided I should try it."

"Don't you think it's kind of . . . strange?" asked Clara.

"Yeah, like incredibly wacko-strange?" added Dan.

"No," said Rufus, "I don't. It's no stranger than putting on a helmet and pads and smashing into other people."

"Come on, Rufus. Football is the all-American game!" said Dan. "What's ballet? Like Russian or something?"

"I don't know," said Rufus. "The names for the positions and stuff are French."

"French!" said Dan. "See what I mean? French! Bizarro! You're going to give us scrubs a bad name, talking French and wearing tights."

"You think so?" asked Rufus, looking at Clara and then at Willy.

Willy shrugged. "How can you give the scrubs a bad name?" asked Willy. "I thought that was the whole point—we're already scrubs, so we don't have to care what people call us."

"Sure," said Dan, "take dance, stand on your head in the hallway. Whatever. I don't care." Dan got up and took his tray to the counter.

"He doesn't seem too happy about it," said Rufus. He turned to Clara. "What do you think?"

"You wouldn't catch me taking ballet," said Clara.

"Why not?" asked Willy.

"It's too pink," she answered.

CHAPTER 5

MR. BALLERINA

Coach Stone didn't say anything more about kicking Rufus off the team. So a week later, Rufus played in the first game of the season.

It was not a very fun game for Rufus. Rufus was playing both offense and defense. That was tiring.

On defense, Rufus had a smaller guy blocking him who was always in his way. Even when Rufus knocked this guy completely over, the guy still managed to get himself up and running again.

On offense, Rufus was opposite a guy who was almost as big as he was. When Rufus hit him, the guy sort of just slid around him and made the tackle.

Coach Stone screamed things like, "He went right by you!" and "What were you thinking about? Ballet?"

And Gabe, the tall guy who played quarterback, said, "Come on guys, help me out. Rufus, your man came right through. Don't dance with him! Block him!"

When the team came in at halftime, Coach Stone asked, "What's the matter, Rufus? You miss your tights?"

"Poor Rufus misses his tutu!" said Biff.

"I told you, I don't wear a tutu," said Rufus.

The Bears were already losing big-time. During the second half, Dan and Willy were put in on defense. By then, even the other team had started kidding Rufus.

"Hey, we're coming right through you, Mr. Ballerina," they said to him.

After one play, the guy who was supposed to be blocking Rufus suddenly gave
him a shove. "You grabbed my jersey,
man," he told Rufus angrily.

"Did not!" said Rufus.

"Did so!" yelled the opposing lineman,
and he shoved him again.

"Get him, Rufus!" yelled Dan. But
Rufus just shrugged and walked away.

"What's the matter with you, Rufus?"
asked Dan. "You going to let that guy get
away with that? You should have slugged
him!"

"I don't believe in fighting," said Rufus.

After the game, Coach Stone told them how badly they had played.

"You've got to be tough!" he said, looking right at Rufus. "You've got to be willing to mix it up! This is football! It's not tiptoeing through the tulips! It's not 'Here We Go 'Round the Mulberry Bush'!"

Rufus kicked at the gravel as they walked to the bus. "Oh, man," he said to Willy. "What does he think this is, the NFL?"

CHAPTER 6

FOOTWORK

On Monday, Rufus sat down at lunch
with his friends. Clara had on a purple
headband that reminded Rufus of the
coach's angry face.

"I'm going to quit ballet," Rufus told
them.

"Why?" asked Willy.

"You know why. Everybody's nagging me. Especially Coach."

"You can't quit, Rufus," said Dan.

"Are you serious?" asked Rufus. "You practically told me to quit!"

"Yeah," said Dan with a shrug, "at the beginning. But it's too late now. I mean, if you quit now, it would look like you gave in to Biff and the Coach—to all those jerks. You can't do that. That would be wimpy."

"The coach isn't a jerk," said Willy.

"He's sure being a jerk to Rufus!" said Dan.

"I thought you guys wanted me to quit, too," said Rufus.

"Not anymore," said Dan.

"Dan's right," said Clara. "Don't give up now."

"You guys are so confusing!" Rufus complained, putting his head in his hands.

Still Rufus was tempted to quit ballet. It didn't seem to be helping. He was as clumsy as ever. The class wasn't that great, anyway. The little girls were all much better than he was.

That night, Rufus asked his parents about it.

"We already paid for the classes," said his mother. "But if you really hate it, you can quit."

"I don't hate it," said Rufus. "It's just . . ." And then he told them about how Coach Stone and the other players were giving him a hard time about it.

"Coach Stone hasn't been keeping up," said Rufus's father. "I know there's at least one pro football team that has signed its players up for ballet lessons."

"Really?" asked Rufus.

"Really. Pro basketball teams, too. It's a big trend. Improves their balance, their footwork. Makes them better players."

"I can't tell any difference," said Rufus.

"It takes time," said his father.

"I'm not sure I'm learning that much. I'm never going to get any good at it anyway."

His mother smiled. "It doesn't matter if you never get good," she said. "What matters is that you get *better*."

"And that he has fun," added Rufus's father.

"Okay," said his mother. "But sometimes you have to get better first. Sometimes the fun comes later."

"Hope the fun gets here before too long," said Rufus.

CHAPTER 7
LIFTS

On Friday, when Rufus was supposed to leave for ballet class, Coach Stone was right in the middle of explaining something about the game the next day.

Rufus didn't want to miss it. So he stayed at practice and was late for ballet class.

Rufus rushed into class and found an empty spot at the *barre*.

"I'm glad you made it," whispered the little girl behind him. "I was afraid you'd quit."

"Why would you care?" Rufus asked.

"It's more fun with you here."

"Thanks." Rufus was surprised. He hadn't thought the girls cared one way or the other.

They turned around and switched feet on the *barre*.

"I know it's a pain," the little girl said. "I mean, my dad giving you a hard time and everything. But don't listen to him."

"Your dad?"

"Yeah. My dad's Coach Stone. I'm Emily Stone."

Rufus was surprised. Emily didn't look like the Coach. And he'd never thought of Coach Stone being a father.

"Hi, Emily," he said.

"You know, it's better if you turn your foot this way," said Emily. "And remember to keep your knees straight."

"Okay," said Rufus. "I'll try."

When class was over, Emily pointed to a poster on the wall. It showed a male dancer lifting a ballerina high over his head.

"That's called a lift," she said. "I jump, and you make the jump go all the way up. Want to try?"

"Sure, I'll try," said Rufus.

So Emily ran and jumped, and Rufus lifted her up over his head.

When he put her down, Rufus looked over at Ms. Farine. He expected her to be mad. But she looked like she was trying not to smile.

"If you're going to do lifts," Ms. Farine said, "you should bend your knees. I'll show you."

Pretty soon, Rufus had a whole line of

little girls wanting to be lifted.

At first it was easy, they were so light. But by the time his mother picked him up, Rufus's arms were sore.

"See you Monday!" said Emily as they left.

From then on, Emily gave Rufus helpful hints at every class. Rufus was glad she did. It made him feel like he was learning something.

And at the end of every class, Rufus did lifts for all the girls in class, over and over.

The girls loved it. And Rufus had to admit, it was pretty fun for him, too. It made him feel like a giant, like Superman or something. Even though he wasn't the one doing the flying.

CHAPTER 8

BIFF SCORES

The Bears lost the second game of the season, too. But this time, they only lost by one touchdown.

The third game was also close. They were losing seven to six at the half. In the third quarter, the Bears received the kickoff and started on a long march down the field.

Rufus was blocking a guy who was just as big as he was, but not any quicker. The guy couldn't get around him. Nobody told Rufus he was doing a good job. But no one was yelling at him, either.

They were down on the ten-yard line when the quarterback, Gabe, called another play to Rufus's side. "But, Rufus, listen," said Gabe in the huddle, peering up from under his helmet. "I want you to let that defensive tackle in, okay? One of us will get him. Just get the linebacker, okay? Go for the linebacker."

"Okay, Gabe. Got it."

It worked. Rufus let the defensive tackle go by and caught the linebacker by surprise. Rufus got in one good hit before the linebacker dodged around him. By that time, the linebacker was too late.

Biff had gone by him and scored the touchdown.

After the play, almost the whole team mobbed Biff in the end zone, congratulating him. Everybody in the stands was cheering for him.

Rufus felt kind of let down.

He turned away and almost ran into Gabe. Gabe slapped Rufus on the back.

"Yeah," was all Gabe said. Then Gabe went up to Biff, and they exchanged high-fives.

CHAPTER 9

THE RAMBLING QUARTERBACK

The Bears won that game, and then they lost another. It kept going back and forth like that.

Willy and Dan were happy because they got to play a lot of defense. The coach wasn't yelling at Rufus any more than at anybody else. It would have been a fun season, except that Coach Stone was so worried about it.

Before the final game, the team's record was four wins and four losses. Four and four. The last game would decide whether the Bears had a winning or a losing season.

The players got to the locker room extra early. No one said much while they suited up. When they were ready, Coach Stone called, "Okay, guys, gather 'round."

With a clattering of cleats on the concrete floor, the team crowded together on the benches.

"This is the last game I'm ever going to coach here," said Coach Stone. His face wasn't purple today. It wasn't even red. It was almost white. His voice was low as he went on. "So we're going to give it our all, right? We're going to give it every last ounce of everything we've got, right?"

Coach Stone paused to look around. Rufus tried to look really serious.

"The other team," said Coach Stone, "the Falcons, aren't that good. But they have one really good player. He's what they call a rambling quarterback."

Coach gave a worried frown as he went on.

"He can pass, and he can run the ball, too. He'll ramble around until he finds an opening. If we can contain him, we'll win. If we can't . . . But I know we can. Right? Right. Okay, let's go."

Coach Stone was right about the rambling quarterback. Rufus felt he was spending the whole game running around the other team's backfield, trying to tackle the guy.

Everybody was having the same problem. Some plays went on so long that Rufus got two or three tries at him before the quarterback finally threw a pass or decided to run the ball. The quarterback faked people out so badly they fell flat on their faces trying to change direction.

Sometimes they were completely sure they had him. They would close in on him from all sides—and then he'd squiggle right through their outstretched fingers.

Coach Stone screamed and turned purple, for a while. That didn't seem to help. Then he quieted down and his face turned back to white again.

He tried everybody on defense. Willy and Dan got to play a lot. When Rufus missed a tackle, the coach took him out. But everybody was missing tackles, so he put Rufus in again and left him in.

At halftime the score was tied: 14–14. Coach Stone didn't have much to say.

"The offense has got to keep scoring," he said hoarsely. "And on defense—we've got to wear that guy out!"

Rufus sat in the shade and drank some water. He wanted to make sure he wasn't the guy who wore out first.

CHAPTER 10

DANCING MAN

In the second half, *everybody* seemed worn out. Even the spectators seemed tired of cheering. Nobody scored in the third quarter. Then, finally, Gabe managed to break away and score a touchdown. The Bears missed the extra point, but still they were ahead, 20–14.

"I did my part! Now you've got to hold them!" Gabe yelled as the defense came out.

"You've got to stop them!" shouted Coach Stone. His voice was cracking.

"Hold them!" screamed the crowd.

"Get him, Rufus!" yelled Rufus's mom and dad.

Rufus tried. They all tried. But the Falcon quarterback was so hard to catch. He passed, he ran the ball, and the Falcons marched down the field. Soon they were on the ten-yard line. First and goal to go.

"We can't let them score," said Willy.

"We'll stop them," said Dan.

Rufus didn't say anything. He was breathing too hard.

On the first play, the Falcons gave the ball to their fullback, who got tripped up and only gained two yards.

On the second play the quarterback took the ball and ran around the far end. Rufus ran after him. Rufus knew he was too slow to catch him, but sometimes—

Yes! The defensive end had come up, so the quarterback had to cut back. He ran— *BOOM!*—right into Rufus. They both fell down.

Rufus had never heard the crowd cheer so loudly. The Falcons didn't gain anything. They still had eight yards to go.

The third play was endless. The quarterback went back to pass. Willy and Dan and two other guys were running around in the backfield trying to catch him. At the same time, the Falcons' fullback and halfback tried to block them.

Rufus hung back a little, trying to make sure their quarterback couldn't run the ball past the line of scrimmage. Finally, the rambling quarterback tried to run. Rufus barely touched him with his fingertips as he scooted past.

Luckily, the linebackers had come up. Willy and Dan were chasing the quarterback from behind. Together, they dragged him down.

He'd gained five yards. Three yards to go. The fans were yelling and screaming from both sides now, making one big wave of noise.

On the last play, the Falcons lined up as close together as possible. As soon as the ball was snapped, they formed a tight wedge. They all moved forward together.

Rufus side-stepped around the Falcons' front line and ran in behind the wedge.

The fullback was there to block him. Rufus ran straight into the fullback—and then Rufus spun around. He did a *pirouette* right around the fullback!

And there was the quarterback—with the ball. Rufus grabbed him from behind, picked him right off the ground, and tossed him back, away from the goal line.

That was it. They had stopped the Falcons! Final score, 20–14. The Bears had a winning season!

"Great game, Rufus!" everybody said.

"Way to get that guy."

"It was so cool when you spun around."

"How'd you get strong enough to pick him up like that?"

Coach Stone was so hoarse he couldn't say anything. He just went around patting everyone on the back. He even gave Rufus a hug.

Back in the locker room, even Biff couldn't think of anything particularly nasty to say. "For a few seconds there," said Biff, "it actually looked like you knew how to play football."

"That wasn't football," said Rufus. "That was ballet."

CHAPTER 11

TOO TRUE

At lunch on Monday, people were still talking about the football game.

"I'm glad I got to see the last quarter," said Clara. "You guys all played well. And maybe I'll have to take up ballet or something. You did a great job, Rufus."

"I bet it won't help for wrestling," said Dan.

"It might," said Rufus. "Remember last year when I lost a takedown by tripping over my own feet?"

"So, are you going to keep taking ballet this winter?" asked Willy.

"Nah, I don't think I will," said Rufus.

"Maybe it was good that you took ballet," said Dan. "But I'm sure glad to hear you're going to quit. I'm tired of all those 'tutu' jokes."

"That's right, no more ballet," said Rufus. "Ms. Farine suggested I sign up for tap dance instead." Rufus started tapping his feet under the table.

"Tap dance!" said Dan, shaking his head. "Man, can't you do something besides dance? Why don't you come rock climbing with me?"

"Isn't that dangerous?" asked Willy.

"Nah, it's almost *too* safe," said Dan. "We always have a rope from the top. If you fall, the rope catches you. Like my instructor says, 'Fall seven times, stand up eight!'"

"I'm not sure I'm brave enough to fall even once," said Rufus.

"Are you kidding?" said Dan. "You've got more guts than all of us put together.

You didn't see any of us taking ballet, did you?"

"That's true," said Willy. "It takes a brave scrub to wear tights in public."

"Yes," agreed Rufus. "That's 'tutu' true to argue with."